THE
SPOOKY
STORYBOOK

Full of Fearsome Fun!

HUTCHINSON

LONDON SYDNEY AUCKLAND JOHANNESBURG

First published in 2001

1 3 5 7 9 10 8 6 4 2

This edition © Hutchinson Children's Books 2001
Text and illustrations © individual authors and illustrators; see Acknowledgements

The authors and illustrators have asserted their right under
the Copyright, Designs and Patents Act, 1988,
to be identified as the authors and illustrators of this work

First published in the United Kingdom in 2001 by
Hutchinson Children's Books
The Random House Group Limited
20 Vauxhall Bridge Road, London SW1V 2SA

Random House Australia (Pty) Limited
20 Alfred Street, Milsons Point, Sydney
New South Wales 2061, Australia

Random House New Zealand Limited
18 Poland Road, Glenfield
Auckland 10, New Zealand

Random House South Africa (Pty) Limited
Endulini, 5A Jubilee Road, Parktown 2193, South Africa

The Random House Group Limited Reg. No. 954009

A CIP catalogue record for this book
is available from the British Library

ISBN: 0 09 176839 X

Printed in Hong Kong

CONTENTS

Jean Baylis

TITCHYWITCH

One afternoon at tea time Sally Smith looked out of the window and saw the most extraordinary sight. Through the sky flew three witches on broomsticks. And on the middle one sat a tiny little witch holding on to her hat in the wind.

"Mum!" screamed Sally Smith. "Come and look. There are witches flying through the sky and they're coming this way!"

"Don't be silly," called Mrs Smith from the kitchen. "You really must learn to stop making up stories."

But Sally Smith knew what she had seen with her own eyes and if you read this story you will find that every word she said was true.

"Here we are," said Warlock, getting off his broomstick. "Number 22. Not bad, is it?"

Titchywitch pulled a face. "Well, I suppose it's all right for a house," she said. "But it's not half as nice as our cave."

"No," said Big Witch with a sigh. "But now they've cut down our forest and built a road over our home, we'll just have to try to live like humans. And that's that."

The family walked into the kitchen.

Titchywitch gasped with disappointment. "But it's horrible! There're no spiders or bats, or anything."

"Never mind, never mind," said Warlock, who seemed to be rather more pleased with the house than anyone else. "We'll have it looking like home in no time."

Usually witches sleep in the daytime and go out on their broomsticks at night. But that evening Warlock announced that they would all go to bed at night, just like humans.

Titchywitch sulked all the way through supper and refused to eat her snail shell and nettle soup. She was absolutely certain she would never, ever, like living in a house, even if she lived to be 932 years old.

Lying in her hammock, Titchywitch found it impossible to sleep. Mum and Dad could pretend to be humans if they liked. But she was going out on her broomstick, and that was that.

Sally Smith was lying in bed when she heard a voice coming from the next door garden.

"Double bubbles, boils and troubles," it said.

She put her slippers on and crept downstairs and into the garden. Standing on her toes, she looked over the top of the hedge. There was a tiny little witch standing in the garden. "I knew it!" she said to herself.

Sally crawled through the gap in the hedge. "Are you a real witch?" she asked.

"Of course," replied Titchywitch crossly. "And I suppose you're a real human." She poked Sally with her finger. "You're all warm," she said.

Titchywitch explained about the house and how she hated it. And how everything was the wrong way round and back to front. "I've got hundreds of troubles," she said. "I was just doing a spell to turn them into toads, when you interrupted me." She held up her arms.

"Double bubbles, troubles be toads.

Double bubbles, toads be troubles."

All of a sudden the garden was full of slippery, slimy toads, croaking at the tops of their voices.

"Now I can fly off on my broomstick," she said. "If you promise not to tell, I'll show you how."

Titchywitch took Sally into the garage. There were two big broomsticks side by side. "These are Mum's and Dad's," she said. "Mine's only a baby one, but it can go quite fast. Do you want to go for a ride?"

"What, now! In my nightie, at night?" asked Sally Smith.

"Of course," said Titchywitch. "But as there are two of us we'd better go on Mum's. I know how to ride it." And before she knew what she was doing, Sally was sitting behind Titchywitch on the big broomstick.

"Stars and moon and night-time sky,
Make my broomstick fly, fly, fly!"

And Big Witch's broomstick rumbled and shook and zoomed off into the sky at astonishing speed.

Up and up they flew.

"Oh dear," said Titchywitch. "It's going too fast."

"Make it go slower!" said Sally.

"I'll just twiddle this thing," said Titchywitch, turning a knob on the front.

But the broomstick seemed to go even faster and soon they were so high above the clouds that they couldn't even see the earth.

"You don't know how to work it, do you?" screamed Sally, almost in tears.

"No, not really," admitted Titchywitch. "We're in trouble now!"

Round and round they whooshed like a rocket on fireworks night. Sally had a sick feeling in her tummy like the time she went on the big dipper at the fair.

Then, all of a sudden, Titchywitch called out, "I've remembered!"

She pulled the brake. The broomstick rattled and shook, slowed down and steadied itself. The girls had a chance to look around.

"Ooh," gasped Titchywitch. "I've never been up this high before."

They were so close to the stars they could almost touch them. Down below they could see the lights of the town twinkling. It was lovely.

Once Titchywitch had mastered the broomstick it was great fun. They went backwards and forwards, forwards and backwards. Then they tried flying upside down.

"Can we fly to my house?" asked Sally. "So I can wave to Mum."

Back on earth, Mrs Smith was putting away the dinner things when she happened to look out of the window. She blinked once and she blinked twice.

Had she really seen Sally flying past the window? ON A BROOMSTICK!

"Oh, dearie me!" cried Mrs Smith, rushing out of the door in her slippers.

Outside the most astonishing sight met her eyes. On the pavement stood a witch, and by her side a big warlock.

"Come down at once," he shouted, waving his cloak about furiously.

"That's my Sally up there," screamed Mrs Smith. "Do something!"

But the broomstick kept on going. Up and up and then down and down and round and backwards and sideways and forwards.

"There's nothing for it," said Big Witch quietly. "You'll have to use the spell."

"Moondust, stardust above the town,
Catch these girls and bring them down."

He threw up his arms and a great whoosh of pink stardust shot up into the sky, enveloped the broomstick and gently carried the two naughty girls down to earth.

They landed with a bump in Mrs Smith's front garden. Sally looked up at Mum.

"I told you there were witches living next door," she said.

Then everyone started to speak at once.

No one noticed Titchywitch and Sally creep off by themselves to the back garden. There wasn't a toad to be seen.

"Looks like all my troubles have gone," said Titchywitch, "now that you're my friend."

And suddenly she thought it wasn't going to be so bad living in a house after all.

Michael Ratnett

MARMADUKE AND THE SCARY STORY

Illustrated by June Goulding

Marmaduke, Jessica and Harriet were all very excited. Grandma and Grandpa were coming to stay.

"Stop fidgeting," said Dad. "Go and do something."

"Yes," said Mum. "Why not paint them a picture as a surprise?"

"Wow," said Marmaduke, as the rabbits raced up to their room. "What a great idea! I'll paint them a wonderful picture!"

"And so will I," said Jessica.

"Me too," said Harriet.

Soon they were very busy.

"No peeping!" said Marmaduke.

When they came back down, they showed each other their pictures. Jessica had painted a picture of a butterfly . . . Harriet had painted a picture of a flower . . .

And Marmaduke had painted a picture of a MONSTER!

"Oh, Marmaduke," said Mum, "why couldn't you paint something nice like the others?"

"Pooh!" said Marmaduke. "Nice things are no fun. I like scary things!"

"Look what we've got for you!" said the three small rabbits as soon as Grandma and Grandpa arrived.

"Why, what lovely pictures," they said. "We can't think which one we like the best!"

Then they all sat down to tea. Grandpa had eleven biscuits.

"Doesn't Grandpa eat a lot!" whispered Jessica.

"It's called being greedy," said Grandma.

After tea Jessica said, "Tell us a story, Grandpa."

"Of course I will," he said. "But I'll just have one more biscuit first."

"Tell them a story now," said Grandma. "You've had quite enough biscuits for one day."

"What sort of story would you like?" asked Grandpa.

"A SCARY story!" said Marmaduke.

So they huddled around, and Grandpa told them a scary story about a monster with three legs, just like the one in Marmaduke's picture.

"Time for bed," said Dad. And they were monsters all the way up the stairs.

It was a dark and windy night.

"What did you think of Grandpa's story?" said Jessica.

"It was a very scary story," said Harriet.

"Yes," said Marmaduke, "but I wasn't afraid. Were you?"

"No," said Jessica.

"Of course not," said Harriet.

But they couldn't get to sleep.

Suddenly Jessica said, "W-what's that noise?"

"What noise?" said Harriet.

"Th-that's just the wind," said Marmaduke.

"Or – or a tree branch tapping," said Harriet.

They listened again.

"It's not," said Jessica. "It's coming from the stairs!"

"W–what shall we do?" said Harriet. "I'm scared!"

"One of you must go and look," said Marmaduke.

"You go and look," said Jessica. "You're the one who likes scary things!"

"All right, we'll all go together," said Marmaduke.

Shivering from the tips of their ears to the ends of their toes, they climbed out of bed and crept towards the door. Marmaduke went in front firmly grasping his cricket bat.

When they were on the landing, they looked down. There, coming up the stairs was a huge shadowy figure!

Thump, thump, click, it went. Thump, thump, click . . .

"It's the three-legged monster!" stammered Marmaduke. And he raised his cricket bat way up high . . .

. . . and hit the monster thwack on the head!

"Ow!!" yelled Grandpa. Then the light came on.
"What is all this noise?" said Dad.
"Marmaduke hit me on the head!" said Grandpa.
"We thought he was a monster!" said Marmaduke.
"Well, he is sometimes," said Grandma,
"especially when he creeps about
after biscuits."
And they all laughed.

Mum made everyone a mug of steaming cocoa
and sent the three small rabbits back to bed.

"I still think you were very brave, Marmaduke," said Jessica.

"I do too," said Harriet, "even though Grandpa wasn't really a monster."

But Marmaduke was busy.

"ROAR!" he screamed!

Franz Hohler

THE LITTLE SCOTTISH GHOST

Illustrated by Werner Maurer

Once upon a time there was a little ghost who lived in a castle in Scotland. His parents were not as young as they used to be, and they were getting rather tired of haunting. So they showed Little Ghost all the things he had to do to frighten people.

First of all, Father Ghost gave him lessons down in the cellar. He showed him how to glide mysteriously along corridors, how to put his head through a wall, and how to make things move from one place to another.

When they had practised long enough, Father Ghost took Little Ghost out haunting for the first time.

"Today," he told Little Ghost, "we are going to glide mysteriously in the great hall with axes stuck in our heads."

When Father Ghost passed the fireplace, the lord and lady of the castle were scared out of their wits. They clung tightly to each other.

But when Little Ghost passed by, doing just the same, they laughed like anything, and they felt perfectly all right again.

"Well," said Father Ghost afterwards, "you'll have to learn to be weirder and more spooky."

Next day, Mother Ghost showed Little Ghost how to haunt the linen cupboard and get in between the sheets, so as to scare the laundrymaid when she came to fetch clean sheets for the beds.

The laundrymaid was scared stiff at the sight of Mother Ghost, and she went straight off to fetch the lady of the castle.

When they both came back to the linen cupboard, they found Little Ghost there, trying to frighten them.

"Oh, look! A little ghost!" said the lady of the castle. "How sweet!" And she went to fetch her husband.

But when they came back, Little Ghost had disappeared.

"Where has he gone?" cried the lady of the castle.

Then the suit of armour behind them slowly raised its arm. But when it was at shoulder height, it dropped again, the suit of armour fell to the ground with a clatter, and Little Ghost toppled out, with some nasty cuts and bruises.

Luckily the lady of the castle had plenty of ointment and sticking plaster to make Little Ghost better, and he was soon well enough to go back to his mother and father.

"Well," said Mother Ghost, when he was back home again, "you'll just have to learn to be even weirder and more spooky." And Little Ghost promised to do his best.

"Right," said Father Ghost, the next evening, "now I'll teach you how to haunt the castle with balls and chains. That always works wonders."

He stood at the top of the stairs leading down to the great hall, fastened two heavy balls and chains to his feet, and then, moaning horribly, he shuffled downstairs and right across the hall, finally disappearing up the chimney.

The lady of the castle was pale with terror, clutching the lord of the castle, who was clutching the back of his chair.

Little Ghost thought that was fun.

As soon as Father Ghost was back, he fastened the balls and chains to his own feet and set off. But the balls and chains were so heavy that they rolled downstairs, out of control, taking Little Ghost with them.

They went all the way through the hall, crashed through a window pane, and landed in the castle moat, along with Little Ghost himself.

And if Mother Ghost had not been on the spot, having guessed something of the sort might happen, Little Ghost might have been drowned.

"Was I any good that time?" he asked, when he was nice and dry again.

"No," said Father Ghost. "You made a lot of noise, that's all. You must learn to be really weird and spooky!"

"But how?" asked Little Ghost.

"I know!" said Father Ghost. "We'll send you to the weirdest, spookiest spook in all Scotland for haunting lessons. He lives in Whistlefield, and you can start tomorrow."

Next evening, when the train stopped at Whistlefield Station, the engine driver just popped his head out of the window of his cab, shouted, "Whistlefield!" and popped his head straight back in again.

No one got out, except for Little Ghost, and as soon as he was there on the station's tiny platform the train went on again.

The castle stood up above a little village, and as Little Ghost walked through the village he could see all the people looking out of the windows. But suddenly terror came over all their faces, and they hurried away from the windows. A dreadful, long-drawn-out whimpering sound could be heard coming from the castle, more of a wail really, and it was so loud that it made the houses tremble.

Little Ghost jumped for joy. "I'm sure
I shall learn how to haunt in a really
weird, spooky way here," he thought,
and he ran to the castle as fast as he
could go.

He knocked at the castle door, but
it was shut, and no one came to open
it. So he crept in through a cellar
window, and started looking for
the Whistlefield Ghost.

But there was no
sign of him.

Little Ghost decided
to call out. "Hullo!" he
shouted. There was a
dreadful howl behind
his back. It made the
whole cellar tremble,
and when he turned
round he saw the
Whistlefield Ghost.

"Who are you?" asked the weirdest and spookiest spook in all Scotland, in hollow tones.

"I'm a little ghost," said Little Ghost, "and I'd like to have some haunting lessons from you, because you're the weirdest and spookiest spook in all Scotland."

"Oh," said the Whistlefield Ghost. "Well, you gave me a nasty fright."

"Will you give me lessons?"

"All right. You can start tomorrow night."

Little Ghost waited impatiently all that night and all the next day. He explored the whole castle, and found that there was no one living there any more.

When he looked down at the village, he saw that the people were very frightened; they walked about all hunched up, and they often glanced furtively at the castle.

When evening came at last, he went down to the cellar where he had met the weird, spooky ghost, and shouted out, "Hullo!"

"Oooooh!" cried the weird Whistlefield Ghost, howling so loud that he made the window panes rattle.

"How do you manage to wail in such a scary way?" asked Little Ghost.

"Because I'm so scared."

"I thought it was you who scared other people."

"No. I'm the one who's scared. I'm so scared that I wail with terror."

"What are you scared of?" asked Little Ghost.

"I'm scared of the least little sound. I'm afraid it might be a weird, spooky ghost or something. You come over to the castle with me, and you'll see what I mean."

They went up the cellar steps together, and as they were about to go through the door to the entrance hall, the Whistlefield Ghost said, "Watch out, this door creaks dreadfully."

And he pushed the door open. It certainly creaked badly, but the Whistlefield Ghost didn't howl or wail. "Aren't you scared this time?" asked Little Ghost.

"No," said the weird and spooky Whistlefield Ghost, "and it's the first time I haven't been scared of that noise. How odd! Watch out: the wind will come howling down the chimney now. It's a very scary sound."

Sure enough, the wind did come whistling down the chimney, but the spooky Whistlefield Ghost did not move a muscle.

"Aren't you afraid of that either?" asked Little Ghost.

"No," said the weird Whistlefield Ghost. "I'm not afraid of that either, not this time. I can't understand it. When I'm on my own, I'm always scared."

The weird Whistlefield Ghost showed Little Ghost all sorts of other places which were usually very spooky and scary, like the dungeons and the castle battlements and the wine cellar.

"I know what it is!" said Little Ghost. "It's because you're not alone. Once I've gone again, you can carry on being scared and weird and spooky."

"True," said the weird Whistlefield Ghost, sadly. "Couldn't you stay a bit longer?"

"Yes, all right," said Little Ghost.

He stayed several more days, and the old Whistlefield Ghost did not make any more weird noises, because he was not scared now, and so the people down in the village were not scared any longer, either.

They ventured to come out of their houses and start work again.

When Little Ghost had been there a few weeks, the village people came up to the castle to set it to rights, sweep away the cobwebs and air all the rooms.

And when Little Ghost wrote to ask his parents if they would like to move to Whistlefield too, they said yes, they thought that was a good idea.

So they came.

And there was a big party up at the castle for all the village people.

And the funniest bit of the whole party was when Little Ghost showed everyone how he had tried to learn to haunt.

John Richardson

THE DREAMBEAST

Deep in a dark distant forest lives the Dreambeast.
He sleeps in the morning, he plays snakes and
ladders in the afternoon . . .

...and he brings the children their dreams at night.

One day the Dreambeast couldn't sleep. He lost every game of snakes and ladders. "Bother!" he said, and grew very grumpy and cross.

"Bother," he grumbled as he set off on his night rounds.

"Bother," he called to the moon as he flew past.

That night he couldn't find any good dreams to put in little Tom's head.

First Tom dreamt that there was
nothing to eat but cabbages . . .
and cabbages . . . and cabbages.

Then he dreamt that everyone had
forgotten him at Christmas.

Next he dreamt a terrible blizzard
blew his favourite teddy away!

Tom jumped up in bed and cried, "MUM!"

Mum came and kissed him better. She shook her fist at the night crying, "Naughty Dreambeast! You should be ashamed."

The Dreambeast was sorry for what he had done. He sat in his den feeling tired and sad, but still he couldn't sleep.

That night he went to Tom
again. Tom dreamt of a sad
Dreambeast who couldn't sleep.
In his dream he captured the
beast and taught him his own
bedtime secrets.

He shared his teddy
and his mug of milk and
his enormous comfy quilt.
Then he read the
Dreambeast a story.

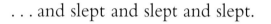

Back in his den, the Dreambeast made
a quilt of wool. He found his old teddy
and boiled up a mug of milk with a
little honey . . .

. . . and slept and slept and slept.

When he woke up he danced for joy.

That night Tom dreamt of merry-go-rounds; of candy sticks and lollipops.

He dreamt that he flew through clouds of blue, and over trees with peaches and pears.

He dreamt of a giant birthday cake and of a party with everyone there.

And he dreamt of that old Dreambeast as he waved him a fond farewell.

Nicholas Allan

THE GHOST OF HILLTOP HOSPITAL

It was midnight at Hilltop Hospital. The moonlit ward was full of shadows.
Suddenly a voice cried, "Help!"

Nurse Kitty ran quickly to Timmy Rabbit's bedside. "What is it, Timmy?"

"I dreamt I saw a . . . g-g-ghost," stuttered Timmy.

Kitty told him not to be scared. "There's no such things as ghosts."

Just then the ward doors opened and the Teds, the ambulance drivers, entered. Kitty told them about Timmy's nightmare.

"Try to be brave, Timmy," said Ted.

"Yer," said the other Ted, who was helping a tiger with a plastered leg. "Like Stanley 'ere."

"Gosh," said Kitty, "Stanley the famous jungle explorer. You must be ever so brave."

"Oh, not really," said Stanley, "I feel quite at home in the jungle, actually."

"We'll put 'im next to Timmy so 'e can fight off the ghost," laughed Ted.

In the staff room, Dr Matthews was telling Dr Atticus about his nightmare.

"HORRIBLE it was!" said Dr Matthews. "It was all about Surgeon Sally. I asked her for a date and . . . she burst out laughing!"

Dr Atticus told him he shouldn't be so afraid and Dr Matthews had to agree. "In fact, the very next time I see Sally . . ." he began. "Aaargh!"

"What's the matter, Matthews?" said Sally, as she walked in. "You look as if you've seen a ghost."

The very next night there was another cry in the ward. This time Timmy said he really had seen a ghost – one without a head.

"No 'ead?" said Ted.

"Actually, he did have a head," said Timmy. "He was carrying it under his arm!"

Dr Matthews told Timmy not to be scared – it was just a silly dream.

"You wouldn't be afraid of ghosts, would you, Stanley?" he asked the tiger.

Stanley replied that even he had fears. He didn't tell them that he was afraid of hospitals because he'd never been in one before.

No one believed in the ghost. The following evening, however, Kitty was walking down the corridor when she heard some ghostly sounds. She turned a corner and out jumped the Teds.

"Oh, you!" she cried and the Teds giggled.

After Kitty left, there were more ghostly sounds.

"You can't scare me with those noises," said Ted.

"I'm not making any noises," said the other Ted.

And it was then that they both saw the Ghost of Hilltop Hospital.

"I told you there was a ghost," said Timmy, as the Teds sat in the ward, trembling.

"Now, don't panic," said Kitty.

Everyone had gathered round, wondering what to do. Then Stanley told them that in the jungle he had learnt that if you have a fear, you mustn't run away – you must chase it. There was only one thing they could do about the ghost – catch it!

Later, everyone was sitting round a table, carefully studying a plan of the hospital. After much thought, Stanley looked up. "What we need," he said, "is a ghost trap."

"I know who could make one," Timmy said excitedly, jumping up. He took Stanley down to the basement. Stanley grew anxious, but Timmy told him not to be afraid, they were just going to visit Arthur and Clare, the lab mice.

"There," said Arthur, when he'd finished making the ghost trap.

"Wonderful!" exclaimed Stanley. "Funny though, it looks just like a mouse tr— I mean, a trap for catching something else."

"Oh no. It's a ghost trap. Couldn't be anything else," insisted Clare.

Soon Stanley and Timmy were off again, to look for a ghost detector. They found one in the operating theatre, where they also found Surgeon Sally.

"We need to detect the ghost," said Timmy.

Sally told them the machine was a scanner, not a ghost detector. "It sends out sounds, which bounce back and form pictures on a screen," she said.

"So it could detect a ghost," Timmy argued.

"Well, I suppose it could," Sally agreed.

Everything was ready. Stanley outlined the plan. Timmy and he would set the trap "here", Dr Matthews and Sally would detect the ghost "here" and Dr Atticus would lead the ghost to the trap with cheese "there".

"Synchronise bleepers," ordered Stanley.

"Synchronising bleepers," said everyone else.

Night fell. There was silence in the ward; not a snore, nor a purr, nor a buzz.

"I wish I were as brave as you," whispered Timmy, as they set the ghost trap. It was then that Stanley told him about his fear of hospitals, and how, thanks to Timmy, he'd lost it.

"Gosh!" said Timmy. "In that case, I'm not going to be frightened of ghosts."

Surgeon Sally and Dr Matthews were hiding in a cupboard with the scanner. It was dark but cosy in there; so cosy that Dr Matthews almost asked Sally for a date. But just then, a figure appeared on the screen of the scanner. "Ghost!" hissed Sally, and pressed her bleeper.

Stanley and Timmy turned off the light and crouched down behind the laundry trolley. They could hear the ghost approaching, getting closer and closer.

Suddenly the trap went SNAP!
"We've caught it!" cried Timmy.
"Roaring success!" said Stanley.

Timmy switched the lights on and ran across to the trap. "But . . . but . . . it's Dr Atticus!" he cried.

"He must've been sleepwalking," laughed Stanley. "That's why we couldn't see his head. Are you all right, Dr Atticus?"

"No, I'm not!" His head popped out. "I'm starving. Can't you hear my tummy rumbling? Where's my cabbage?"

Stanley picked it up off the floor. "Here it is. Don't lose your head about it!" And everyone laughed.

The following morning, Dr Matthews found Sally inspecting the laundry schedule. It was his great chance to ask her out and, to his amazement, she agreed.

"I've been meaning to ask you for ages," he admitted. "I've just been too scared. But after last night, I thought it was silly to be afraid."

"It's certainly silly to be afraid of ghosts," she said. "Everyone knows they don't exist."

Dr Matthews agreed.
When Sally had gone, however, he saw the laundry sheet move. Suddenly it rose up into the air. He yelped and ran, not noticing that the shape of the ghost was very like the Hilltop ambulance drivers!

Dyan Sheldon

A WITCH GOT ON AT PADDINGTON STATION

Illustrated by Wendy Smith

It was raining. The bus was crowded. The passengers were tired. The conductor was grumpy. The driver wanted to go home.

A witch got on at Paddington Station. The conductor told her, "Leave that broom with the pushchairs, love."

The witch sat down. She smiled at the people around her, but they didn't seem to notice.

But the witch was very happy. She liked riding on buses. She liked the ticket the conductor gave her. She liked to ring the bell when her stop came.

In a very loud, bright voice the witch said, "I'm going to visit my sister. I'm taking her some presents." No one seemed to hear her.

In a louder, even brighter voice the witch said, "I'm going to visit my sister. I bought her a new broom."

The conductor came up and the witch told him that she was going to visit her sister.

"That's forty pence," said the conductor.

The witch was very happy, and when she was happy she liked to sing. She began to sing. Everyone looked at her. Then everyone looked at the conductor. The witch sang even louder.

"There's no singing on this bus," scowled the conductor.

Everyone looked at the witch. She thought they must like her song. The conductor pulled the cord and the bus stopped. The conductor said, "Either get off this bus or stop singing."

The witch looked surprised. "But I'm going to visit my sister," she said.

"Not on this bus, you're not," said the conductor.

The driver came into the bus.

"What's going on?" he asked the conductor.

"I'm going to be late for my tea," the witch replied. "I'm going to have tea with my sister."

"Let's get moving," ordered the driver.

"Yes," shouted the other passengers, "let's get moving."

The conductor picked up the witch's bag. "Off," he commanded.

"But I'm going to visit my sister," protested the witch. "She's expecting me."

The conductor pulled one side of the bag. The witch pulled the other.

"Leave off," shouted one of the passengers. "Let her have her bag."

"Let's get going," yelled another passenger. "I don't have all day."

Soon several people were pulling at the bag. Passengers were standing in the aisle, screaming at one another.

The bag broke.

There was a blue moon. There were pink stars.
There was one fountain. There were two toucans.
There were three parrots. There were four kittens.
There were five garden gnomes.

Flowers grew up from the floor. The birds sang. A parrot sat on a boy's shoulder. A garden gnome threw an old woman a kiss. A star fell into the driver's pocket. Everyone looked at the witch.

"These are the presents I'm taking to my sister," smiled the witch. "Do you think she'll like them?"

Everyone looked at the conductor.

"'Ere," said the conductor, "we can't have this on my bus."

A kitten rubbed against his leg. Butterflies sat on the passengers' shoulders. Everyone was smiling or laughing.

The witch didn't hear him. She had a big blue teapot in her hands and a stack of blue cups and saucers. "Anyone for tea?" she asked.

"Well . . . a . . . oh . . . thank you," said the driver, taking a cup of tea.

"What are you doing?" roared the conductor. "You can't drink tea on this bus." Someone stuck a biscuit in his mouth. "We've got a timetable to keep," he spluttered.

"Don't be daft," laughed the passengers. "It's raining, isn't it? You can't have a timetable in the rain."

"That's right," said the driver, "everything slows down in the rain."

The conductor pulled a bunch of daisies from his pocket. "This is against the rules," he shouted.

But no one was paying any attention. They were all having tea.

"'Ere," yelled the conductor, "we're meant to be in Victoria right now."

The witch smiled. "And here we are," she said, gathering up her things. "This is where I get off, at Victoria Station. I'm going to visit my sister. She's expecting me for tea."

David Cox

CAPTAIN DING
THE DOUBLE-DECKER PIRATE

Illustrated by Graham Round

I've been standing here for a million years! thought Stan. Mum has turned into stone. And the others have all turned into trees . . . WON'T THE BUS EVER GET HERE?

Suddenly, a bus came trundling along the horizon. But it looked strange . . .

Instead of being RED, this bus was BLACK.

As the black bus approached, you couldn't help noticing that where the number normally was, there was a picture. Stan squinted to make out what the picture was.

A SKULL and CROSSBONES! He looked at Mum. She was still made of stone.

The bus stopped, and on the platform stood an amazing character.

"Well bless my soul! A new shipmate!"

"You look like a pirate," said Stan.

"Look like, my boy? I am! I'm CAPTAIN DING, THE DOUBLE-DECKER PIRATE. The most feared pirate on all the number seven bus route."

"I thought pirates were at sea, and had ships," said Stan.

"Aha! That was in the old days, my boy. Most pirates did have ships, but now there aren't many ships left, and the pirates have to rob each other because there's not enough treasure to go round . . . And besides, I get seasick! So what do you say? Do you want to join my busload of bandits and go in search of adventure and treasure?"

"Will my mum still be here when I get back?"

"If she's waiting for a red bus, she'll be there for ages yet!"

Captain Ding gave Stan a ticket. As he took it, a huge cheer went up. He looked down the bus and, to his amazement, saw Alex, Jack and Billy from school.

The pirate bus sailed off down the High Street . . .

"Where are we going?"

"To capture some treasure, young Stan."

"What, like gold and diamonds?"

"Don't be daft boy. We're after chocolate, and lots of it!"

The bus came to a sudden halt outside what looked like the supermarket, but somehow it was . . . different.

"Now then you young pirates, here we are. Only a few hundred feet from Chocolate Island."

"Chocolate Island? That's only the supermarket, the boring old supermarket. I've been here a million times with my mum, and it's the most boring place in the world."

Stan was beginning to suspect that Captain Ding wasn't quite the pirate he liked to think he was.

All at once, Captain Ding stepped inside the supermarket and started emptying soap powder packets onto the floor.

"Now shipmates, grab some bottles of fizzy water and shake 'em up. We'll show doubting Stan here just how boring the super-market isn't. Now open your bottles!"

The fizzy water sprayed and splashed everywhere.

"Quick, now each of you jump into a shopping trolley."

Within seconds the fizzy water had mixed with the soap powder to make . . . a sea of bubbles!

"Now we're a fleet. Follow me, I know just where Chocolate Island is. But be on the lookout. All seas are dangerous, even bubble ones."

As they sailed along the aisles, Stan's trolley shook. There's something down there, thought Stan. I hope it's friendly.

It wasn't. A long, squiggly wormlike thing rose up out of the bubbles. Then another, and another.

"SPAGHETTIPUSSES!" yelled Captain Ding.

A fierce battle instantly started.

A long, wiggly spaghetti arm gripped Stan. Captain Ding sprang into action, grabbing the waving monsters in his big pirate hands. Captain Ding wrestled with the Spaghettipusses until at last he had tied them all into a big knot.

"That'll teach them to mess with Captain Ding and his chocolate-hunting shipmates!" he cried. Everyone cheered.

"Onwards pirates, Chocolate Island is just around the corner."

Chocolate Island was in fact the sweet counter. But it looked just as magical as Captain Ding made it sound.

All the Greats were there. The chewy chocolate, the bubbly chocolate, the chocolate with two hazelnuts in every bite. There were even kinds of chocolate Stan had never seen.

"Well blow my braces! I've never got this far before," said Captain Ding. They loaded the chocolate into an empty trolley.

At that moment a snowball flew from the frozen food counter and hit Stan full on.

"Uh-oh, I thought we were doing too well, me hearties," moaned Captain Ding.

A strange humming filled the air. Captain Ding looked very worried.

"What is it Captain?"

"Shipmates, there's something I forgot to tell you about . . . or rather someone."

"Who Captain, who?"

"Admiral Cod and his band of Goody-Goodies."

"I've seen him on telly, selling fish fingers and singing that rotten song," said Stan.

"Right you are my boy, and a right wet blanket he is too. He won't let us capture the chocolate without a fight. He'd lose his cushy job prancing around the supermarket smiling at mums."

"Hand over the chocolate Ding, you scruffy bus driver!" came a gravelly voice.

Stan and his classmates grabbed lettuces, ready to do battle against snowballs on Captain Ding's command . . .

"Attack!"

The snowball and lettuce battle raged for ages, with neither side getting the upper hand. Then, with a sneaky look in his eyes, Admiral Cod roared:

"Sing the song!"

The Goody-Goodies and Admiral Cod sang:

"We are so fine,

We are so good,

We always do just as we should,

We couldn't be more goody-good!"

It was worse than a thousand cats yowling. Captain Ding and his crew tried to cover their ears, but the Goody-Goodies' polished teeth glared into their eyes. It was hopeless, they turned and sailed away as quickly as possible.

Without any chocolate.

Back on board the bus everybody was glum.

"Never mind, we can go back another time. With earplugs and dark glasses," said Captain Ding.

They arrived at Stan's bus stop. Mum was still made of stone.

"There, what did I tell you Stan? You've been out, had an adventure, come back, and your mum's bus still hasn't turned up. Oh well, I suppose I'd better get going. Got to drop off the rest of the crew."

He pressed the bell twice and suddenly . . .

. . . the bus in front of Stan was an ordinary red one!

"Come on Stan, stop daydreaming," said Mum, who had suddenly come to life.

"But I'm a double-decker pirate! Where's my black bus?"

Then he saw that the trees had turned back into people again.

"Get on the bus Stan, I don't know, you're in a world of your own half the time," flustered Mum.

Stan felt very confused on the way home.

But just as they walked into the house, a scrunched-up piece of paper fell out of Stan's pocket. He undid it. It was a picture of a skull and crossbones.

His pirate bus ticket! Below the picture it read: THIS TICKET IS VALID ON ANY PIRATE BUS ADVENTURE/RAID WITHIN THE DING ZONE – providing you're not a Goody-Goody!

Shiver me timbers! I wonder when my mum's going shopping again? thought Stan, as he climbed upstairs into bed.

Michael Ratnett

PETER AND THE BOGEYMAN

Illustrated by June Goulding

"Don't do that," said Peter's grandad. "The Bogeyman will get you."

"Have you ever seen the Bogeyman, Grandad?" said Peter.

"Of course," said Peter's grandad. "He's seven feet tall; he's got five arms, and he wears a cloak with a hood to hide his face."

"Just look at the mess you've made!" said Peter's grandma. "It would serve you right if the Bogeyman got you."

"Have you ever seen the Bogeyman, Gran?" said Peter.

"Certainly not," said Peter's grandma. "I was always too good. But I know all about him.

He sneaks up on naughty children and scares them stiff. And if that doesn't do any good, he uses his most powerful spell and turns them into salt, and carries them back to his castle to flavour his soup."

"Have you ever seen the Bogeyman, Mum?" said Peter.

"There's no such thing as the Bogeyman," said Peter's mum. "He's just something made up to scare children into being good. Who's been filling your head with all that nonsense?"

Peter thought and thought about the Bogeyman.

And the more he thought, the more it seemed that if the Bogeyman were real, then it was time that somebody did something about him.

So he made his plans.

On Monday he was quite naughty.

On Tuesday he was very naughty.

On Wednesday he was
very, very naughty.

And on Thursday he was a
complete disgrace!

"The Bogeyman must be coming for me now or never!" he said on Friday.

And that evening, when he went up to bed, he carried a big cardboard box with him.

It was a dark, dark night. Peter waited in bed with his torch at his side.

As the town clock struck midnight, the window of Peter's room was raised by a silent hand. And in climbed a shadowy figure.

It was seven feet tall; it had five arms, and it was wearing a hood and cloak.

It was the BOGEYMAN!

Peter waited and waited until the Bogeyman was right in the middle of the room. Then he shone the torch straight in his eyes.

"AARGH!" went the Bogeyman, covering his eyes because the light hurt so much. He staggered forwards.

Then Peter pulled the carpet away, and the Bogeyman fell flat on his back.

"AARGH!" went the Bogeyman, furious at being tripped up. He began to crawl towards Peter.

Peter hurled a bag of flour in the Bogeyman's face. SPLAT!

"AARGH!" coughed the Bogeyman, who had never been made to look so silly before.

Then, as he wiped the flour from his eyes, Peter pulled a string, and a great big net dropped over the Bogeyman.

He was trapped!

97

"AARGH! AARGH! AARGH!" roared the Bogeyman, who was now very, very, very angry.

He tore the net to pieces. Then he raised himself up to his full height, and gathered up every last bit of his magic. And with a TERRIBLE yell he threw his most super-duper ten times ordinary strength extra-powerful salt spell right at Peter!

But, quick as a flash, Peter pulled out a mirror and sent the spell bouncing right back at the Bogeyman.

ZAPFIZZPOP!

The Bogeyman instantly turned into a statue of salt!

"And that's the end of you," said Peter.

On Monday, when Peter went to school, he took the Bogeyman statue with him.

He entered it in the Art Competition.

Everyone thought that it was very good, and the judges awarded him Second Prize.

His friend Susan came First with her Plasticine kangaroo, even though its tail was a bit wobbly.

"Well done," said Peter's mum and dad. "But what is it?"

"It's the Bogeyman," said Peter.

"But there's no such thing," they said.

"Not any more," said Peter.

Peter gave the Bogeyman statue to the school cooks to flavour the children's soup. And they didn't have to buy any more salt – not for a whole year!

Nicholas Allan

THE MAGIC LAVATORY

Jeffrey lived with his house-proud Aunt Julia.

She was so house-proud that he wasn't allowed to play with toys, or friends, in case he damaged the furniture.

One day he opened up his great-great grandfather's cabinet. His great-great grandfather had been an inventor.

Inside he found a bottle of Thick Yellow Goo, and on the label it said "100% PURE MAGIC, USE WITH CARE".

Jeffrey poured the Goo into some cups and spoons. This is what happened:

Suddenly Aunt Julia came in.

She was so angry she snatched the bottle and poured all the Goo down the lavatory.

Then she sent Jeffrey straight to bed.

That night Jeffrey thought about the Thick Yellow Goo. Early next morning he was still thinking about it when, from the bathroom, he heard some noises; some gurgling, spluttering, bubbling noises.

Something strange was going on in there . . .

And it got stranger . . .

. . . and stranger.

Jeffrey crept out of bed just in time to see something creep out of the bathroom.

At first Jeffrey was afraid, but the "something" looked friendly.

It also looked hungry.

Jeffrey gave it some bread. But it didn't like that, so he gave it some of Aunt Julia's plates which it did like – very much.

It ate the cutlery, and the kitchen table, then wandered round the house chomping and chewing . . . A nibble here, a nibble there . . .

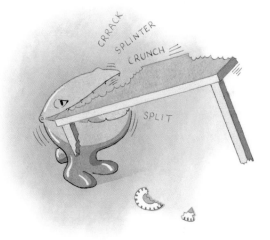

It ate:

A vase

A piano

A lampshade

A picture

A Persian carpet

A brooch

A chest-of-drawers

A sofa

Two armchairs

A Louis XIV
carriage clock

A washing machine

A hair dryer

A dishwasher

A potted plant

A colour television

and . . .

AN AUNT.

When the house was empty they did a little dance. Jeffrey was so pleased with his new friend.

They chased each other and played basketball and hide-and-seek. After that they went out and scared people . . .

. . . which was great fun.

Finally they went to a railway station and caught a train. They had a wonderful ride all the way to the seaside.

Jeffrey's friend loved water and flushed with excitement when it saw the sea.

They went for a quick dip together.

Afterwards, they lay in the sun to dry. Jeffrey bought an ice lolly and gave his companion the wrapper to eat.

Then he told some very rude jokes, which made his friend gurgle and splutter with watery laughter.

Towards the end of the afternoon they walked back to the station and caught the train. It had been a day to remember.

When they arrived home, Jeffrey's friend began to feel tired.

Jeffrey realised the Yellow Goo was running out . . .

Very slowly his friend started to change back into its old self. Jeffrey was sad.

Suddenly he felt very alone.

But just then an
amazing thing happened.
Its mouth began to open.
And out stepped . . .

Aunt Julia!

She seemed none the worse for wear. In fact she was so happy to be back and to see Jeffrey again she didn't care about the house any more – not even the Louis XIV carriage clock.

From then on Jeffrey and Aunt Julia lived happily together.

And Jeffrey was allowed to play whenever he liked!

Tony Ross

THE SHOP OF GHOSTS

"Tell me a story Grandad. It's Christmas Eve and I can't sleep."

Grandad crinkled his face and tickled his nose. Outside, the snow had begun to stick and sounds were muffled.

"I don't know any stories," he grumbled. "Not REAL ones."

"NO stories are real!" I said.

"Some are realer than others," Grandad replied. "When I was a lad, something happened . . . but I can't say whether it was real or not . . ."

We were both quiet for a moment. Outside, footsteps crunched by; inside, the shadows listened as the old man went on.

"It happened at Christmas-time too, but it was when the world was different. It was when to ride on the top of a tram was to be on a flying castle . . .

It was when you could buy nearly all the best things in the world for a penny – except smiles and starry nights, thunderstorms and cosy toes – things like that you could get for nothing! But you know what I mean. You could get a mouthful of sweets for a penny.

Well, I came across a crooked little toyshop, hiding in the back alleys of the city. Although the street was dark, the window was ablaze with the colours of a hundred toys. They reminded me of the children who bought them . . . bright, if just a little grubby. I have always thought though, that brightness is more important than cleanliness, because brightness is about the heart, and cleanliness is only about soap!

As I pressed my nose against the glass, I began to fall into a strange dream that shut out the dreary street and the grey houses. The shop window became a brightly lit stage. It seemed that the little objects were small, not because they were toys, but because they were far away.

The tin bus was really a city bus, bumping its way across a desert on its way to the station. The wooden elephant was really a wild animal, and the black doll a magnificent prince, leading his court across a flaming land. A Noah's Ark was a huge lifeboat, red in the light of the sun, at the start of a new life.

Behind me, the other people in the grimy street hurried silently on, as if I and the shop weren't really there.

The shop seemed lost in a magic fog. Half in a dream, I went in and tried to buy a band of tin soldiers.

The man in the shop was very old and bent, with confused white hair. Although he looked ill, there was no suffering in his eyes; he looked rather as if he was falling quietly asleep.

He gave me the soldiers, but when I put down the money, he blinked, and pushed it away.

'No, no,' he said feebly, rubbing his eyes. 'I never take money, never have. I'm rather old fashioned you know. I've always . . . given presents. I'm too old to stop now.'

'Good heavens!' I said. 'You can't run a shop like this. Why, you sound just like Father Christmas!'

The old man blew his nose.

'I am Father Christmas,' he said.

No sounds came from the street outside, and the glowing shop window failed to lighten the shadows in the room. I don't know why, but something made me say, 'You look ill, Father Christmas.'

'I am dying,' he said. I did not speak, and it was he who spoke again.

'Nobody wants me anymore. They are all full of science. They say that I am too jolly, that I make people dream and give them ideas. They even say that I am not real. How can I not be real? How can I be too jolly? I don't understand. These modern people are living, and I am dying.'

'No!' I replied. 'They may well be alive, but THAT'S not living.'

Father Christmas and I looked sadly at each other for some moments when, in the utter stillness, I heard a rapid step outside in the street. The next moment, a figure dressed in the strangest old-fashioned clothes flung itself into the shop.

The newcomer did not seem to see me, and he fixed the old man with a surprised stare.

'Great jumping lizards!' he cried, his arms whirling like a windmill. 'It can't be you! Say you're not you! Why, I came here to ask where you were buried.'

'I'm afraid I'm not dead yet, Mr Dickens,' said Father Christmas with a feeble smile. 'But I am dying.'

'But great dithering dodos, you said you were dying when I was a lad!' said Charles Dickens, dancing on his toes. 'And you don't look any different now!'

'I've felt like this for a long time,' said Father Christmas sadly, sinking down into his old chair. I held my breath in the shadows. Mr Dickens turned his back, and poked his head out of the door, into the darkness.

'Charlie!' he shouted. 'He's still alive!'

Somewhere in the muffled alleys, a beggar cat squealed and a voice roared, 'Out of my way, Tomkins. Splendid news! I must see for m'self.'

Another apparition appeared in the doorway, and a large gentleman in an enormous wig

came in, waving his sword wildly and cutting the tops off the feathers of his own hat. His face was proud, almost sneering, but he had the eyes of a naughty puppy dog. He seemed to grow and fill the shop.

'Indeed,' he roared. 'This is marvellous.' I jumped back as a ghostly sword whistled by. 'This Father Christmas was dying when I was on the throne. How CAN he still be here?'

'This must be King Charles the Second,' I thought, my senses reeling, as the King's laughter rattled the night.

The room darkened and seemed to fill with more ghostly newcomers, all peering at Father Christmas. I kept well back in the shadows.

'And why art thou still here?' whispered an elf-like man dressed in black. (I think he was William Shakespeare.) 'Gadzooks! He looks twice as grey but methinks he told me years ago that he was going to die.'

I also thought I heard a green-clad man, like Robin Hood, say in words so odd I could hardly understand, that he knew Father Christmas under the greenwood tree, and that he had said he was dying then.

The old man smiled sadly, and still nobody noticed me.

Shakespeare and Robin Hood looked accusingly at Father Christmas, who only hung his head.

'I have felt like this for a long time,' he said in his feeble way.

Charles Dickens suddenly leaped across to him.

'Since when?' he asked brightly. 'Since you were BORN?'

'Yes . . .' said the old man, wringing his hands. 'I have always been dying.'

Dickens took off his hat with a flourish, like calling an audience to cheer. 'I understand it now . . .' he cried, '. . . YOU WILL NEVER DIE.'"

I don't remember falling asleep, or Grandad turning off the lights, but I dreamed about his story, in a mixed up way – of Robin Hood riding a blue elephant through the snow on Christmas Eve.

I do remember waking up early on Christmas morning and pulling the pillowcase full of presents, rustling and bumping in that exciting way, over my bed. As the Christmas paper was torn away, and the joys revealed, there was a step on the landing, and my bedroom door creaked. It was only Grandad, with a breakfast tray. He winked.

"Is Father Christmas dead, then?" he whispered.

"'Course not!" I replied, and I winked too.

ACKNOWLEDGEMENTS

The publishers gratefully
acknowledge the following
authors and illustrators:

Titchywitch published by Hutchinson Children's Books
© Jean Baylis 1988

Marmaduke and the Scary Story published by Hutchinson Children's Books
Text © Michael Ratnett 1990 Illustrations © June Goulding 1990

The Little Scottish Ghost published by Hutchinson Children's Books
© Verlag Sauerländer 1979 Translation © Hutchinson Children's Books 1980

The Dreambeast published by Hutchinson Children's Books
© John Richardson 1988

The Ghost of Hilltop Hospital published by Random House Children's Books
Text © Nicholas Allan 2000 Illustrations © Nicholas Allan 2001

A Witch Got on at Paddington Station published by Hutchinson Children's Books
Text © Dyan Sheldon 1987 Illustrations © Wendy Smith 1987

Captain Ding published by Hutchinson Children's Books
Text © David Cox 1992 Illustrations © Graham Round 1992

Peter and the Bogeyman published by Hutchinson Children's Books
Text © Michael Ratnett 1989 Illustrations © June Goulding 1989

The Magic Lavatory published by Hutchinson Children's Books
© Nicholas Allan 1990

The Shop of Ghosts published in a fully illustrated edition by Andersen Press and
adapted and illustrated by Tony Ross from an original story by G. K. Chesterton
© Tony Ross 1994